## THAT'S WHEN POSEY
## HEARD A SOUND. . . .

Woof! . . . Woof! . . . Woof!

A dog!

The people next door had a dog! Posey was so excited. She jumped off the swing and started across the yard. Posey stopped. It sounded like a big dog. A very big dog. And it had a very deep voice. Like a giant's voice. Posey's eyes opened wide. What if it was a giant dog? A giant, jumpy dog like the one in the park? And it didn't like little girls?

WOOF! . . . WOOF! . . .

Posey didn't wait to hear the third, giant WOOF! She ran.

# OTHER BOOKS YOU MAY ENJOY

# PRINCESS P🌼SEY

### and the

# NEXT-DOOR DOG

Stephanie Greene

ILLUSTRATED BY

Stephanie Roth Sisson

PUFFIN BOOKS
An Imprint of Penguin Group (USA) Inc.

PUFFIN BOOKS

Published by the Penguin Group

Penguin Young Readers Group, 345 Hudson Street, New York, New York 10014, U.S.A.

Penguin Group (Canada), 90 Eglinton Avenue East, Suite 700, Toronto, Ontario, Canada M4P 2Y3
(a division of Pearson Penguin Canada Inc.)

Penguin Books Ltd, 80 Strand, London WC2R 0RL, England

Penguin Ireland, 25 St Stephen's Green, Dublin 2, Ireland (a division of Penguin Books Ltd)

Penguin Group (Australia), 250 Camberwell Road, Camberwell, Victoria 3124, Australia
(a division of Pearson Australia Group Pty Ltd)

Penguin Books India Pvt Ltd, 11 Community Centre,
Panchsheel Park, New Delhi - 110 017, India

Penguin Group (NZ), 67 Apollo Drive, Rosedale, Auckland 0632, New Zealand
(a division of Pearson New Zealand Ltd)

Penguin Books (South Africa) (Pty) Ltd, 24 Sturdee Avenue,
Rosebank, Johannesburg 2196, South Africa

Registered Offices: Penguin Books Ltd, 80 Strand, London WC2R 0RL, England

Published simultaneously in the United States of America
by G. P. Putnam's Sons and Puffin Books, divisions of Penguin Young Readers Group, 2011

9 10 8

Text copyright © Stephanie Greene, 2011
Illustrations copyright © Stephanie Roth Sisson, 2011
All rights reserved

THE LIBRARY OF CONGRESS HAS CATALOGED THE G. P. PUTNAM'S SONS EDITION AS FOLLOWS:
Greene, Stephanie.
Princess Posey and the next-door dog / by Stephanie Greene ;
illustrated by Stephanie Roth Sisson. 1st ed.
p. cm.
Summary: Holding her princess wand, six-year-old Posey
finds the courage to visit the large dog next door.
ISBN: 978-0-399-25463-5 (hardcover)
[1. Dogs—Fiction. 2. Fear—Fiction.]
I. Sisson, Stephanie Roth, ill. II. Title.
PZ7. G8434Pq 2011
[Fic]—dc22 2010028012

Puffin Books ISBN 978-0-14-241939-7

Design by Marikka Tamura
Text set in Stempel Garamond

Published simultaneously in Canada. Manufactured in China by South China Printing Co. Ltd.
Printed in the United States of America.

# CONTENTS

# BIG EXCITEMENT

There was big excitement in Miss Lee's class. Posey ran up to Nikki and Ava as soon as they got to the room.

"Luca has a new puppy!" she said. "Come see the picture!"

There was a crowd of children around Luca. Everyone was pushing to be in front.

"Let me see!" they all said. "Let me look!"

"He's so cute," said Posey. "Wait till you see."

But Ava and Nikki didn't get to see.

Miss Lee clapped her hands. "Boys and girls," she called in her pay-attention voice. "I need all of you to sit at your tables, please."

Everyone hurried to sit down.

"I know you're excited about Luca's puppy," Miss Lee said. "So we will hold our class meeting now. He can tell us about it."

All of the kids sat in a circle on the rug in front of the Word Wall. Miss Lee sat in her rocking chair.

"Remember the rule," she told them. "We only ask questions about Luca's dog. We don't tell stories about our own pets. This is Luca's time to share."

It was a hard rule to follow.
Everyone wanted to talk about
their pets, too.

"Go ahead, Luca," said Miss Lee.

Luca stood up. "I got a new
puppy," he said.

He held up a picture. It was a little dog with floppy ears. "His name is Roscoe. He's brown."

Posey rose up on her knees so she could see better. So did everyone else.

"Bottoms, please." Miss Lee waited until they all settled down. Then she said, "Who would like to ask Luca a question?"

Hands shot into the air.

"Nate?" said Miss Lee.

"What kind of dog is he?" Nate asked.

"A mix," said Luca.

Miss Lee called on Maya next.

"Where does he sleep?" she asked.

"In his crate," Luca said.

"Does he cry at night?" Nikki asked.

"Sometimes," Luca answered.

There were so many questions, they ran out of time.

"We have to stop now," said Miss Lee. "It's time for reading."

"Ohhh..." A disappointed sound went up around the circle.

"Here's what we'll do." Miss Lee stood up. "You are all very interested in dogs. So this week, you can write a story about your own dog or pet. Then you can read it to the class."

Everyone got excited again.

Except Posey. She didn't have a pet.

Not a dog.

Not a cat.

Not a hamster.

"Those of you who don't have a

pet," Miss Lee said, "can write about the pet you hope to own someday."

Miss Lee had saved the day!

Now Posey had something to write about, too.

# PAINS IN
# THE NECK

Posey told her mom about Luca's puppy on the way home.

"Everyone in my class has a pet except me," she said.

"I'm sure not everyone," said her mom.

"Well, lots of kids." The ends of Posey's mouth turned down.

"We have talked about this before," her mom said. She parked their car next to the house. "No pets until Danny gets bigger. I have enough to take care of as it is."

Danny was in his car seat next to her. Posey looked at him and frowned.

He wet his diapers. He spit out his vegetables. He made messes.

It was all Danny's fault.

When her mom opened her car door, Posey reached over and pulled his binkie out of his mouth. She hid it behind her back.

Danny let out a roar.

"Posey . . . ?" said her mom.

Posey gave it back to him.
"Sorry, Danny."

Her mom lifted Danny
out of his car seat.
"Maybe you need
some time by
yourself," she said.

Posey went and
sat on her swing.
She didn't pump.
She made marks
in the dirt with
the tip of her
sneaker.

"Hey, Posey!"
a voice called. It was Tyler. He
lived next door. He was playing
soccer with his brother, Nick.

Tyler was in the fourth grade.
Nick was in second. They teased her

all the time. But maybe today they were going to let her play!

Posey ran into their yard.

"You're a big kid now, right?" Nick asked.

"Right," said Posey. "I'm in first grade."

"I don't know," said Tyler. "You still look pretty small to me."

Posey stood up as straight as she could. "I'm bigger than I look," she said.

"Okay." Tyler pointed. "Go stand over there."

Posey ran and stood near a big tree. "Here?" she asked.

"Perfect," said Nick. "Now, don't move."

He and Tyler kicked the ball back and forth. They ran around the yard. They shouted to each other.

"What about me?" Posey called.

"Don't move!" said Tyler.

He gave a great kick. The ball zoomed past Posey. It went into the bushes.

"Game's over!" he shouted. "I win!"

"But I didn't get to do anything," said Posey.

"Sure you did," said Tyler. "You were a great goalpost."

He and Nick slapped each other on the back and laughed.

"Big dummy heads!" Posey shouted.

She marched home. She would do something to show them she was a big kid.

Just wait!

# AN ALIVE PET

The next day, Maya was the first one to read her story to the class.

"My dog is Dash. He chews socks," she read. "One time he chewed my dad's slipper. Now it's Dash's slipper."

She showed them a picture. It was a yellow dog. It had something blue in its mouth.

"That's a good story, Maya," said Miss Lee. "You told us a lot. Anyone else?"

The rest of the class was still working on their stories.

Posey could not get her story started. She wanted to write about a dog, too. But she had a secret.

She was a tiny bit afraid of dogs.

When she was little, a dog jumped on her in the park. It wanted to lick her ice cream cone

and it knocked her down.

Posey could still remember the scary feeling. She didn't want anyone to know.

"I'm writing about my cat, Puffy," Ava said. "She's so soft."

"I'm writing about my gerbil," said Nikki. "What are you writing about, Posey?"

"Why don't you write about Roger?" said Ava.

Roger was Posey's stuffed giraffe. He was blue and white. She got him when she was a tiny baby.

But he was not alive.

Posey wanted to write about an alive pet like everyone else.

"Maybe I'm going to get a real pet," she said.

"Really?" said Nikki. "When?"

"Maybe soon," Posey pretended.

She would wish and wish.

Maybe it would come true.

# THE NEXT-DOOR DOG

Gramps drove Posey home from school. A moving truck was parked in front of the red house next door.

"Looks like you have new neighbors," Gramps said.

"Maybe they have a little girl!" said Posey.

She ran up to her room and put on her pink tutu. She put on her necklace with the pink beads, too. And her magic veil with the stars.

Then she went outside and sat on her swing.

There was a hedge between her yard and the red house. Posey pumped hard so she could see over.

If she went high enough, maybe she'd see a little girl! Maybe the little girl would see her!

See her, Princess Posey, in her beautiful pink tutu. It fluttered up and down with every swing.

But all Posey saw was an empty yard. She stopped pumping.

That's when Posey heard a sound.

Woof . . . Woof . . . Woof.

A dog!

The people next door had a dog!
Maybe she could write her story
about it!

Posey was so excited, she stopped
the swing.

Woof! . . . Woof! . . . WOOF!

Posey froze. It sounded like a big
dog.

A very big dog.

WOOF! . . . WOOF! . . . WOOF!

And it had a very deep voice.

Like a giant's voice.

Posey's eyes opened wide.

What if it was a giant dog? A giant, jumpy dog like the one in the park? And it didn't like little girls?

WOOF!...WOOF!...

Posey didn't wait to hear the third giant WOOF!

She ran.

# YOU CAN'T TELL
# A DOG BY ITS BARK

Tyler and Nick were getting on their bikes in their driveway.

"Hey, Posey!" Tyler called.
"What's your hurry?"

"Did you see a monster?"
shouted Nick.

Posey didn't stop. She ran up
the steps and into the house.

She slammed the kitchen door behind her. Gramps was standing at the stove.

She was safe.

"Is someone after you?" Gramps asked.

He cooked dinner for them every Wednesday. Posey's mom had to work late. Tonight, he was making chili.

The kitchen smelled good. Posey's heart slowed down.

"Gramps, can a little dog have a big bark?" she asked.

"The only little dogs I know are yappers," said Gramps. "Yap, yap, yap, all day long."

"Big dogs are mean, aren't they?" said Posey.

"Not on your life." Gramps dumped a can of beans into the pot. "I had a dog as big as a horse when I was your age. Target was his name. Target's heart was as big as he was."

"They sure *sound* scary."

"Barks don't mean a thing," Gramps said. "If you want to know about a dog, look at its eyes. Kind eyes mean a kind dog."

Posey shivered. She was too afraid to get close enough to the next-door dog to see its eyes.

"Why the questions about dogs all of a sudden?" said Gramps.

Posey told him about the barks.

"I'll tell you what," Gramps said. "You and your mom can go over there on Saturday. You can meet the dog together."

It was a perfect idea. Posey was so lucky to have her gramps.

She threw her arms
around him. She squeezed
as hard as she could.
"I love you, Gramps,"
she said.

"I love you, too," said Gramps. "But watch I don't get chili on your head."

# NOW OR NEVER

Posey told Ava and Nikki about the barks the next day.

"How are you going to write a story about that dog?" asked Ava. "You don't know what it looks like."

"And you don't know what its name is," said Nikki.

"Maybe it's a ghost dog." Ava opened her eyes wide. "Maybe it isn't even real."

"Maybe you heard a ghost bark," said Nikki.

The three girls shivered. They grabbed one another's hands.

"The ghost dog said woof . . . woof . . . woooooooooofffff!" Posey made it sound like a ghost.

Ava and Nikki shrieked. It was so much fun to be scared when they were together.

"All right, girls. Settle down," Miss Lee called.

Nikki ran over to her.

"Miss Lee!" she said. "Posey has a ghost dog next door!"

"You three are being silly," said Miss Lee. "But that reminds me."

She smiled around at the class.

"Tomorrow will be the last day to read your pet stories," she told them. "Everyone needs to finish up today."

Oh, no!

That meant Posey couldn't wait until Saturday. She had to meet her next-door dog today.

Besides, if she went with her mom, Nick and Tyler would think she was a baby.

She had to do it by herself.

Posey made up her mind right then and there.

She was going to go over and see that giant dog as soon as she got home.

# BEING BRAVE

Posey was
ready.

She had on her pink tutu and her magic veil. Posey put on her new belt with purple flowers, too. She held her princess wand in one hand in case she needed magic.

She was Princess Posey.

Princess Posey was brave. She could go anywhere and do anything.

All by herself.

Posey went downstairs. Her mom was folding clean clothes.

"I'm going outside," Posey said.

"Okay," said her mom. "I'll be out in a little bit with Danny."

Posey stood on the back steps and listened. She didn't hear a sound.

Maybe the next-door dog was taking a nap.

That was it!

She would be as quiet as a mouse and peek through the hedge. She could see how big it was without waking it up.

Taking tiny baby steps, Posey tiptoed over to the hedge and looked.

There was a doghouse in the yard behind the red house. It had a fence around it.

Posey heard a small Woof! . . . Woof! . . . Whimper.

What was that?

That's not what it sounded like yesterday.

It sounded like a dog that was crying.

Woof! . . . Whimper . . . whimper.

It was crying!

What if it was hurt? What if it needed her help?

Posey ran all the way around the hedge and into the yard next door. Then she stopped.

A brown dog was lying inside the fence.

It was a giant, all right. It had so much fur, it looked like a bear.

The scared feeling came back to her stomach.

She wanted to help it. She did.

The dog whimpered again.

Whimper . . . whimper . . . whimper.

It was a tiny baby sound. The giant dog didn't seem so giant anymore. It didn't sound as scary, either.

It sounded sad.

Posey tiptoed closer.

No wonder it was crying! Its paw was stuck in one of the holes in the fence. There was dirt all around. The dog had been digging a hole.

The giant dog licked his paw and whimpered.

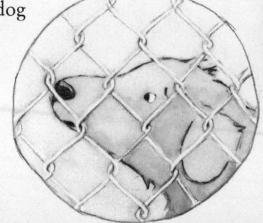

She had to help. She *had* to.

There was only one thing for Posey to do.

CHAPTER
EIGHT

# HERO'S HERO

Posey crouched down. From here, the brown body looked like a huge mountain.

What if she hurt its paw even more? It might growl at her.

Or bite her, even.

Posey jumped up. She shook her head. She squeezed her eyes shut. No, no, no!

She couldn't do it. She was too afraid. Maybe when she was in second grade.

Then the dog gave a quiet woof!

Posey opened her eyes. The dog was looking up at her. It had huge brown eyes.

They were kind eyes.

Sad eyes.

They looked into Posey's eyes and said, Will you help me?

Yes. Posey made up her mind. She could do it.

She knelt down and took the dog's paw in her hands. "You better not be mean to me," she told it sternly.

Then Posey gently pushed the paw back through the fence.

The minute it was free, the dog leaped up.

It shook its big body.

It wagged its long tail.

It wiggled and
waggled and did a
big happy dance.

The dog looked
so funny! It had
dirt on its nose.

The next thing
Posey knew, it licked
her face with its big, slurpy tongue
right through the fence.

*Thank you,*
*thank you,*
*thank you,*
the lick said.

"Yuck," Posey cried. She jumped up. "You have germs, you silly dog."

But she was happy, too.

"He's doing that because you helped him," a voice behind her said. "You're Hero's hero."

# DON'T BE AFRAID

A lady smiled at Posey as she came across the yard. "I'm Mrs. Romero, your new neighbor. What's your name?"

"Posey," she answered. "You live next to me."

"Hello, Posey," said Mrs. Romero. "Hero loves you because you helped him."

Mrs. Romero opened the gate to Hero's pen. Posey followed her in.

"Sit," Mrs. Romero told him.

Hero sat.

"Posey, this is Hero," said Mrs. Romero. "Hero, this is Posey. Shake hands."

Hero held up his paw.

Posey came forward slowly and shook it.

She rested her hand on Hero's broad back. His fur was soft and warm.

"He's just a big baby," Mrs. Romero said. She kissed Hero's

head. "No matter how many times he gets stuck, he keeps trying to dig under fences. Don't you, boy?"

Hero leaned his big body against Posey. She patted his head. When she stopped, he moved his head to ask for more.

"He likes little girls," Posey said.

"Yes, he does," said Mrs. Romero. "He loves all children."

"I'm so glad you moved next door," said Posey.

"Po-sey!" someone called.

It was her mom.

"Can I show Hero to my mom and Danny?" Posey asked.

"Sure. I'll come with you." Mrs. Romero snapped a red leash to Hero's collar. "Would you like to walk him?"

"Oh, can I?"

Posey held Hero's leash and walked him into her yard. He stuck by her side the whole way.

"What a wonderful dog!" her mom said. "Look, Danny! Look what Posey found!"

Danny squealed. He held out his arms.

"His name is Hero," Posey said.

"Posey is *his* hero," said Mrs. Romero. "She unstuck his paw."

Just then, Nick and Tyler came out of their house.

"Can I show them Hero?" Posey asked.

"Go ahead," said Mrs. Romero.

Posey proudly walked Hero across the driveway. Nick ducked behind Tyler when he saw them coming.

"Whoa!" said Tyler. "Is that a bear or a dog?"

"His name is Hero," said Posey. She walked up to them. "His paw was stuck, but I helped him."

"Weren't you afraid?" Tyler asked as he petted Hero's head.

"A little."

"Cool," Tyler said. "See, Nick? Posey doesn't act like a chicken."

Nick stayed behind his brother. Posey could tell he was afraid.

"You can pet him," she told him. "He won't hurt you. He's very gentle. Aren't you, boy?"

She knelt down and wrapped her arms around Hero's neck. He looked at her with his huge brown eyes.

They were filled with love.

They made Posey feel ten feet tall.

She was hugging a dog as big as a bear.

And she wasn't afraid.

# HE'S MY HERO

It was the last day to read pet stories.

"Did you hear the ghost dog again?" Nikki asked Posey.

"He's a real dog," Posey said. "I met him. He's a giant."

"Oh, no!" said Ava. "What did you do? Were you afraid?"

Posey shook her head. She didn't want to tell them. She wanted her story to be a surprise.

"Posey?" Miss Lee said. "You are the last one to read. Are you ready?"

"Yes." Posey picked up her paper. She stood in front of the class.

"Big dogs have big barks," she read. "They go, Woof! . . . Woof! . . . WOOF!"

Everyone laughed.

"A dog moved next door to me."
Posey held her paper tight. "He is
big. But he is gentle."

Last night, she did not know how to spell *gentle*. Her mom wrote it down for her.

"His paw was stuck in the fence. I pushed it out," Posey read. "Tyler said, 'Cool.'"

She turned her paper around so everyone could see the picture she drew.

"This is my next-door dog," she told them. "He helped me be brave. He's my hero."

# P⚘SEY'S PAGES

I made my own beaded necklace. It was so
easy. All you need is a pencil; scissors; glue;
a piece of yarn, elastic, or string long enough
for a necklace; and bright-colored paper
(magazines, wrapping paper, wallpaper).

1. Cut the paper into long,
skinny triangles that are about
one inch wide at the base.

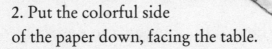

2. Put the colorful side
of the paper down, facing the table.

3. Lay the pencil along the base of a triangle.

4. Hold the edge of the
paper to the pencil and
roll the pencil over one
and a half times.

5. Squirt glue onto the remainder of the triangle.

6. Carefully roll the pencil right up to the tip.

7. Slip the bead off and stand it upright to dry.

8. Paint your beads with clear nail polish to make them shiny! Or use sparkly nail polish to make them fancy!

9. String your beads onto your necklace.

That's all you have to do! I'm going to ask Miss Lee if I can show the whole class.

Love, Posey

P. S. I painted my beads with sparkly purple nail polish. They're beautiful!!!

Watch for the next **PRINCESS POSEY** book!

# PRINCESS POSEY
### and the
## MONSTER STEW

Posey is so excited about Halloween. She doesn't need to carry a flashlight to go trick-or-treating the way she did in kindergarten. But she's a little worried about the monster stew Miss Lee is cooking up.

Thanks to the sparkliest pink costume ever (and her pink tutu, of course!), Princess Posey is ready for any spooky things that might come her way.